This igloo book belongs to:

....

Published in 2014
by Igloo Books Ltd
Cottage Farm
Sywell
NN6 0BJ
www.igloobooks.com

SHE001 0214
2 4 6 8 10 9 7 5 3 1
ISBN: 978-1-78197-813-9

Written by Xanna Chown

Illustrated by Hannah Wood

Printed and manufactured in China

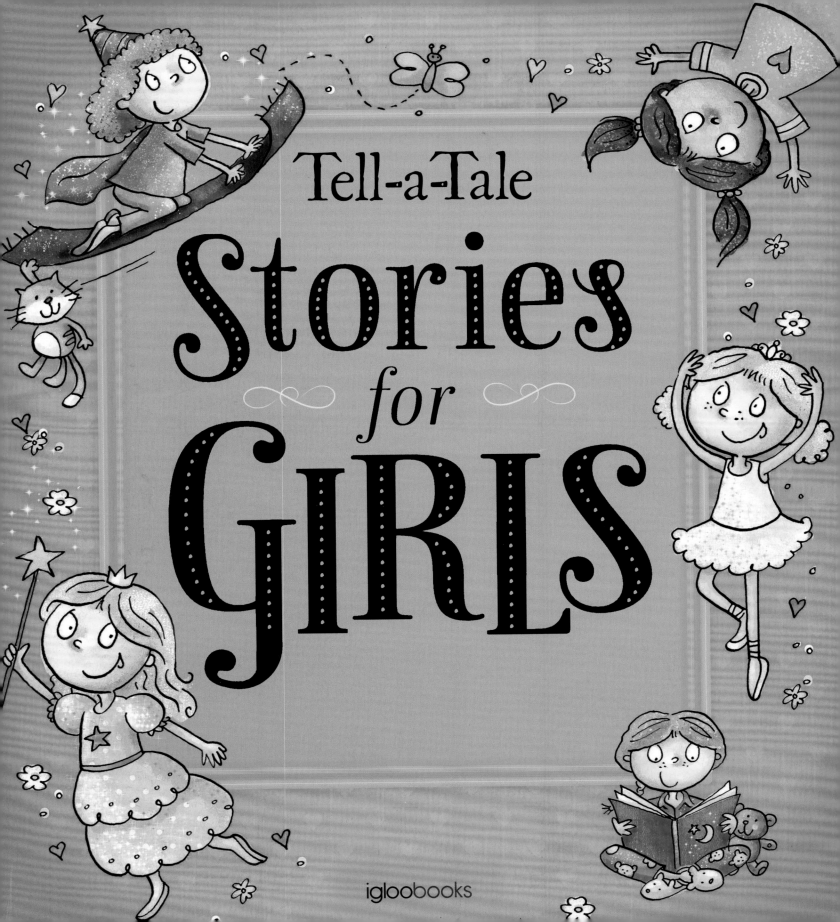

Tell-a-Tale
Stories for GIRLS

igloobooks

Contents

Face Painting Fun

Roxy was really excited. She had been invited to the birthday party of her best friend, Maisie. Roxy rang the bell at Maisie's house and Maisie opened the door with a huge grin. "Meow," she said. "Come in." She was wearing a leotard, with a pink bow around her neck, a long tail and cat's ears.

Roxy went into the house feeling puzzled. Maisie didn't usually dress like a cat. Then, she saw the other guests. Lara was wearing a funny clown outfit and Piper was a ballerina. Lucy, Ellen and Mo were all dressed as fairy princesses.
"Oh, no," thought Roxy, with a sinking feeling. It was a costume party, but she had forgotten to dress up!

"Don't worry," said Maisie, giving her friend a hug. "I've got an idea."
She ran to her room and came back with a pair of fairy wings. "Put these on,"
she suggested. So, Roxy put on the wings. They were pretty, but she didn't
feel very special. There were already three fairies at the party and Roxy didn't
want to be the fourth.

Just then, Maisie's mother opened the door. "Time for the surprise," she said. "Everyone look in the garden!" The children followed her outside and cheered when they saw a huge bouncy castle on the lawn. "Have fun," said Maisie's mum, laughing, as the children raced towards it. "Maisie's dad is making balloon animals and I'm going to do face painting," she added.

"Please can Roxy be first?" said Maisie, taking her friend up to the table where her mum had pots of paint and brushes. "Do you want fairy make-up?" asked Maisie's mum. Roxy shook her head, sadly. "I see," said Maisie's mother, thoughtfully "What else has beautiful wings? I know! A butterfly." Roxy's face lit up. "Yes, please!" she cried. No one else was a butterfly. So, Maisie's mother got out her paints and got to work.

Soon, Roxy's face looked like a glittery butterfly. Maisie found some curly antennae and gave them to Roxy. She fluttered this way and that, giggling. "You look brilliant," said the other girls. Roxy and Maisie jumped onto the bouncy castle and jumped up and down. "I love being a butterfly," giggled Roxy, and Maisie agreed. "Bouncy butterflies are definitely the best," she said.

Ballet Shoes

It was time for ballet class at Silver Steps Ballet School. Florence pulled on her red leotard and took out her pink ballet shoes from her bag. The shoes were very tattered and worn, but Florence didn't mind. She believed they were lucky because she always danced well when she wore them. "I'll never change my lucky ballet shoes," Florence said, slipping them onto her feet.

"Gather round girls," said Miss Silver, the ballet teacher, clapping her hands.
"I have an announcement to make. Silver Steps Ballet School is going
to put on a show and you will all take part."
Florence and her friends started to chatter, excitedly, about dances
and costumes and audiences and lights. It was going to be amazing!

13

At home, Florence told her mum and dad about the show. She put on her lucky ballet shoes and whirled and twirled in front of the mirror. "Watch me, Dad!" she shouted, doing an extra big jump. Whoops! Florence tripped and landed with a thump. "Oh, dear," said her dad, noticing the holes in Florence's shoes. "It's about time you had a new pair of ballet shoes."

14

The next day, when Florence's mum came back from the shops, she had a special surprise. "Dad told me about the holes in your ballet shoes," she said. "You can't wear holey shoes in the show, so I've got you a lovely new pair." The new ballet shoes were beautiful and fitted perfectly, but secretly, Florence was worried. Her old shoes had always been lucky. She couldn't possibly dance without them.

That night, Florence tossed and turned in bed, wondering what to do. Then, she had an idea. She sneaked out of her bedroom and tiptoed down the stairs. She took her new shoes out of her ballet bag and put her lucky shoes in their place. Then, she hid the new shoes under the blanket in the cat's basket and crept back to bed.

16

The next day was the day of the show. "Florence," called her mother.
"It's time to go. You'll never guess where I found your new shoes!"
Florence could guess very well, but she didn't say a word. She waited until
her mother wasn't looking, then dashed out into the garden and tucked
the new shoes behind a pot of sunflowers.

"Whatever are you doing?" asked her dad, making Florence jump.

"These shoes might look great," she explained sadly, "but my old shoes were lucky. I'm worried that if I don't wear them, I won't dance well."

Florence's dad scooped her up into a big hug. "Oh, Florence," he said, laughing. "There's no such thing as lucky shoes. You've practised every day since your last ballet class. You're going to be the star of the show!"

Florence's dad was right. At the show, Florence leapt, spun, twisted and turned in her new ballet shoes. The whole audience clapped and cheered. "Well done, Florence," said her teacher. "Your new shoes must be lucky." Florence smiled and shook her head. She knew now that she was a good dancer, whatever shoes she wore.

Dream Lands

It was a lazy, sunny day and Lola was in the garden reading the last page of an adventure story to her dolly. The story was all about a girl who flew to enchanted lands on a magic carpet. Lola gave a big sigh. She lay down beside Dolly and looked up at the sky. "I wish I could be a girl who goes on adventures," she said.

The warm sun shone and butterflies fluttered past. Lola yawned, cuddled Dolly closer and settled down. The birds twittered sweetly and in the flowerbeds, little bees hummed dreamily, flying from flower to flower. Lola closed her eyes and listened to the soft buzzing of their tiny wings.

Suddenly, Lola felt the rug beneath her starting to shake, wriggle and jiggle. She sat up in surprise and looked down. "Wow!" she gasped. The rug was flying! Her garden was already far below. Lola held on tightly, as the trees and houses whizzed past, faster and faster. "Slow down, rug!" she called.

The rug gave a little shake and slowed down. Soon, they were drifting gently over a meadow, where cute, little teddy bears were having a picnic, eating delicious cakes and drinking cups of fizzy lemonade. "Hello, bears!" called Lola. The bears all smiled as they waved back at her.

The magic rug flew on and soon Lola saw a pink palace covered in yummy sweets. The rug swooped closer and a princess waved from one of the windows. "This is the candy palace," she said. "Would you like some cookie ice cream?" Lola was so surprised, she nearly forgot to say thank you! She gave the sweet ice cream a big lick. It tasted like chocolate chip cookies!

The rug carried Lola far above the candy palace to a land covered in beautiful flowers. Lola had never smelled anything so lovely. Suddenly, the air was filled with fairies. They flew around her, leaving trails of magic sparkles. "We're so excited to see you," said the fairies, in tinkling voices. "We've never seen a real girl before!"

25

Lola played for hours with the fairies. Then, she noticed that the sky was getting dark. It was time to go home. Lola said goodbye and the rug whisked her back to the candy palace. Through the window, Lola saw that the princess was tucked up in bed. In Teddy Land, the bears had packed up their picnics and were heading home. Lola yawned. Her eyes were starting to close.

Suddenly, Lola heard someone calling her name. She opened her eyes and found that she was back in the garden. "Wake up, Lola," said her dad. "You've been asleep for ages. You must have been having a good dream." Lola blinked. "I've been on a magical adventure," she said, with a smile. "Thank you, rug," she whispered.

Josie and Joy

"Josie!" called her mother. "It's seven o'clock. Time to get up!" Josie yawned and stretched, then rolled over in her comfy bed. "I'm asleep," she mumbled. Suddenly, the door burst open and her little sister, Joy, ran into the room. She bounced onto the bed, then dived under the covers and snuggled down. "Me, too!" she shouted.

Josie loved Joy very much, but it annoyed her when her little sister tried to copy her, which was almost all the time. When Josie went to the bathroom to wash her face, Joy came too. She sprayed water on the floor, got toothpaste on her face and soap in her eyes. "Oh, dear," said Josie, giving Joy a comforting hug.

After breakfast, Josie wanted to do some painting. She took out her art box and carefully started to paint a lovely, blue sky. "Me, too!" shouted Joy, clambering onto her sister's lap. *Splosh!* Joy splattered paint onto the paper, the table, the chair and all over her sister's jumper. "You're too little to paint with me!" cried Josie.

Josie cleared up and cleaned her jumper. Then, she sat on the sofa to watch a funny new show on the TV. "Me, too!" yelled Joy, climbing up beside her. "Shh," said Josie. "This is a show for big girls, not little ones." Joy couldn't sit still. She wriggled and jiggled around so much that Josie missed all the best parts of the show.

At lunchtime, Josie helped her mother decorate some cupcakes. She was just piping on some cream frosting, when Joy rushed into the kitchen. "Me, too!" she called, grabbing the bag of mixture and squeezing it. The gooey, sugary mixture splodged out of the bag with a spurt. It went all over Josie, the kitchen cupboard and the floor. "Look what you've done now, Joy," moaned Josie.

Josie went out to the garden to help her dad water the flowers. She held the hose over the flower bed and her dad turned on the tap. *Sploosh!* The water shot out of the hose. "Me, too!" shouted Joy, running towards her and grabbing the hose from Josie, so freezing water splashed everywhere.

Josie was wet from the top of her head to the tip of her toes. For a moment, she felt cross, then she started to giggle. She picked up the hose and sprayed water at her sister, until she was giggling, too. "I've got an idea," said their dad. "Put the hose in the paddling pool and fill it up. Then you can splash as much as you like and it won't matter how wet you get!"

Josie's mum brought out the girls' swimming costumes and some bath toys. They all began to laugh and splosh around. "We've found something you can do together, at last," said mum with a grin. Josie and Joy played happily, all afternoon. Splashing around was great fun for big girls, but it was just perfect for little girls, too!

Mia and Chalky

Happy Hoof Riding Stables

Mia loved living next door to Happy Hoof Riding Stables. Every day, after school, she rushed round to visit the ponies that lived there. The pony Mia liked best was a sweet, old, grey one called Chalky. The stable's owner, Jim, let Mia brush the pony's coat and feed him tasty snacks.

One day, Mia was bringing Chalky a crunchy carrot, when she overheard Jim talking to someone outside Chalky's stable. He sounded very serious. "Yes, I agree," he was saying. "It's time for him to go." Mia felt very upset. Jim was going to give Chalky away! She couldn't let that happen.

Mia waited until Jim and the man had gone. "I've got to save Chalky," she thought. Carefully, she opened the stable door and held out the carrot. "Come on, Chalky," she said. The pony clip-clopped after her, across the yard and down the short path that led to her back garden. "You're safe now," said Mia.

Chalky sniffed Mia's pockets, hoping for another carrot. When he couldn't find one, he gave a snort and trotted over to the vegetable patch. "Oh, no, Chalky," gasped Mia. "Dad will be upset if you eat his vegetables!" She patted the pony's nose and gently pulled him back onto the lawn, his hooves churning the grass into mud as he went.

Next, Chalky saw Mum's prize roses. He thought they looked delicious.
Squish, squash! Chalky trampled over the flower beds in his hurry to get to them.
"No!" shouted Mia and Chalky was startled. He whinnied and ran straight into
Mum's clean washing that was hanging on the line. With a neigh, he shook his
mane and chewed the lovely rose he had just plucked.

Mia dashed into the house to see if she could find any more carrots, but Chalky wanted to follow her. The pony stuck his head through the door and gave a happy whinny at all the exciting food smells in the kitchen. "No, Chalky!" shouted Mia. "You're too big to come in." Perhaps this wasn't such a good idea, she thought.

Mia's mum gasped in surprise. "Mia, why on earth have you brought Chalky into the kitchen?" she asked. "Just look at my clean washing!"

Mia explained what she had heard in the stable. "Oh, Mia," said her mother. "I know you were trying to help Chalky, but it was wrong to take him. I'd better phone Jim and tell him what has happened."

Mia and her mother led Chalky back to the stable where Jim was waiting.
Jim explained that he had been talking to the vet about Chalky. "When I said that
Chalky had to go, I meant he had to go with the vet for some treatment," said Jim.
Mia felt very silly. "I'm sorry," she said and she looked very sad.
"There's no harm done," said Jim and Mia felt much better.
"Nothing that a bit of gardening won't fix," Mum said, and everyone laughed.

The Best Bunny

It was the day before Milly's birthday and she was visiting the pet shop at the end of her road. She loved to see all the different animals that lived there. There were cute puppies, chatty parrots and fish of all shapes and sizes. Whenever Milly went into the pet shop, she would stroke the little kittens because she loved their cute, little paws.

There was one animal, however, that Milly loved to visit more than any other and that was Snowy the white rabbit. "Hello, Snowy," she whispered. "I've come to see you again." The shopkeeper gave Milly some lettuce for Snowy to nibble and she stroked him while he ate. Milly hoped, secretly, that she would get Snowy as a birthday present.

The next day was Milly's birthday. Her dad took her to the shops to buy some balloons to decorate the house. On the way home, they passed the pet shop and Milly popped in to say hello to Snowy. When she got to the hutch, however, Millie was horrified to see the word SOLD in big, black letters.

Milly felt upset, but the shopkeeper was very kind. "I'm sorry that Snowy's not here, Milly," he said, "but don't worry, he has gone to a very good home." The shopkeeper tried to cheer Milly up by letting her feed the fish. Milly scattered flakes of food into all the tanks, but all she could think of was Snowy and she felt so disappointed.

Milly hurried home with her Dad. She wanted to tell her mother all about what had happened, but she was nowhere to be found. Milly looked in the kitchen, the bathroom and the bedroom. "Perhaps she's in the garage," suggested Milly's dad, smiling. Milly was confused. Why would her mother be in there?

Just as Milly rushed outside, she saw the garage door opening. Mum came outside and Mia ran to tell her that Snowy has been sold. Then, Mia noticed that Mum was holding something. It was Snowy! Mum handed the rabbit to Mia. "Happy Birthday," she said.

Milly cuddled Snowy and the soft, little rabbit snuggled into her neck.

"I can't believe he's really mine," Milly gasped. "When the shopkeeper said Snowy had gone to a good home, he meant ours!" Her dad nodded and smiled.

"I'm glad he didn't give the secret away," he said. "After all, what better home could Snowy have than one with you?"

Milly took Snowy out into the garden and let him hop around. The little rabbit hopped here and there, sniffing the flowers with his twitchy, pink nose.

Then, Milly's mother brought out a birthday cake with a sugar rabbit on the top.

"Happy birthday, Milly," said Mum and Dad.

"Thank you," said Milly, cuddling Snowy. "This is the best birthday I have ever had!"

Sam's Sleepover

Getting ready for bed was so much more fun when there was someone to share it with, thought Ruby. Her new friend, Sam, had come for a sleepover and they were both so excited. The two girls giggled as they washed their faces, brushed their teeth and admired one another's pyjamas. They even swapped slippers just for fun.

Ruby and Sam cuddled up under a blanket on the sofa. "Whose old teddy bear is that?" asked Ruby, laughing and pointing to Sam's special bear, Alfie.

Suddenly, Sam felt a bit silly. Would Ruby think she was too old to have a teddy?

"Nobody's," she replied, sadly. Ruby's mum could see that Sam felt a bit upset.

"Drink this hot milk," she said. "Then, I'll read you a story.

After drinking their milk, the girls went upstairs and snuggled into their cosy beds. Mum sat down on Ruby's bed. "Alfie wants to tell you a story," she said. "Once upon a time, there was a princess called Sofia. She had lots of beautiful toys, but the one she loved best was her teddy, Edward. She cuddled him every night."

"One night, Sofia's cousin came to stay at the castle. She pointed at Edward and started to laugh. 'Oh, no,' thought Sofia. 'She thinks I'm too old for a bear.' Then her cousin opened her bag and pulled out her own bear. 'Snap!' she said. The bears looked exactly the same. The princesses laughed and went to sleep, cuddling their bears tight."

Mum said it was time to go to sleep and said goodnight. She quietly tucked Alfie under Sam's quilt. Sam settled down, but it wasn't long before she heard Ruby wriggling and jiggling about. "What's the matter?" asked Sam.
"I can't sleep," whispered Ruby. "I usually cuddle my teddy, but you don't have one, so I felt a bit silly."

Sam put on the light. "Yes, I do!" she cried and she pulled Alfie out from under her quilt. Sam giggled and reached under her pillow. She pulled out a teddy who was old and worn, too. "Snap!" cried the two girls together. Then, just like the princesses in the story, they settled down with their much-loved teddies and had a lovely night's sleep.

The Bridesmaid's Dress

Arianne was so excited, she couldn't keep still. Her big sister, Tara, was getting married and Arianne and her cousins were bridesmaids. Arianne's mother helped them all put on their matching silk dresses and then she got her camera. She told Arianne to stand one side of Tara and her cousins on the other. "You look lovely," she sighed.

58

Suddenly, the doorbell rang, *ding-dong!* "That must be the florist," said Mum. She opened the door and the woman brought in all the flowers for the wedding. She had lots of boxes. "That's far too many!" gasped Tara. "We must have ordered the wrong amount by mistake."

"Can I do anything to help?" asked Arianne. Mum said she should play with her cousins quietly for a while. Arianne's cousins just wanted to read their comics, so Arianne took her paints into the lounge and started to paint. She got a few splodges of blue paint on her dress by mistake, but she was sure no one would notice.

"Are you ready yet?" asked Arianne. She had finished her picture but no one seemed to notice. So, Arianne went out to the sandpit and made a beautiful sandcastle with a little moat. One of the buttons from her dress was a bit loose, so she pulled it off and used it to decorate the top tower.

Arianne went back inside. "Are you ready yet?" she asked again, but Mum said there were still lots of things to do. So, Arianne went back outside and sat on the swing. Whoosh! She swung forwards and backwards, then jumped off and landed with a splat in a muddy puddle. Dirt and mud were splashed everywhere. "Whoops," said Arianne, looking down at her very muddy dress.

"Arianne!" called her mum from the house. "It's time to go." At last, thought Arianne. She smoothed down her rumpled skirt and went back inside. Her cousins saw her and started to giggle. Then, Tara saw her, too. "You can't be a bridesmaid looking like that!" she cried. "Your dress is completely ruined."

"Don't worry," said Arianne's mother. "I've got an idea." Mum got Arianne a cloth to clean her face and hands. Then, she opened one of the boxes of flowers. "Arianne can be a flower girl," said Mum and set to work, pinning the spare blooms in place all around the muddy frock. Soon, Arianne was covered in beautiful, sweet-smelling flowers.

At the ceremony, Arianne had to walk in front of the bride, carrying a basket of rose petals. She threw them on the floor for her sister to walk on. It was a very important job. Her sister was very pleased. "You make a great flower girl, Arianne," she said, "and I'm very glad we found a use for all those extra flowers, too."

The Lighthouse Dolphin

Lily loved staying with her grandad. He lived in a lighthouse near a rocky beach. Each day, Lily would climb to the top of the lighthouse to see if she could see dolphins in the bay below. She loved to watch them splash and play, especially the babies because they were so cute.

One morning, Lily and her grandad were playing on the beach. They were scrambling around the rocks, looking for shells and crabs in the rock pools. Lily had just popped a pink spiral shell into her bucket, when she noticed a rocky cave near the water's edge. "Can we explore in there, please?" she asked her grandad.

Lily's grandad helped her climb over the slippery stones into the cave.
Inside, there were small pools where the sea had swished in and out.
There must be some really interesting shells and crabs here, she thought.
Suddenly, a loud splashing came from one of the pools up ahead. "It would have
to be a very big crab to make that sort of noise," said Lily, feeling a little scared.

"Don't worry," said Grandad. "It's probably just a seagull." Then, they heard a strange sound. *Click-click-click!* "It didn't sound like a bird," thought Lily. Grandad looked around the cave and then gasped in surprise. "It's a cute baby dolphin," he said, smiling. "It must have swum in here, then got left behind when the tide went out."

Lily scrambled over the rocks to take a closer look. "We have to help it get back to the sea when the tide comes in," she said and Lily's grandad agreed.
Lily fetched her towel from the beach and dipped it in the sea. The dolphin's skin needed to be kept wet and cool. "I think I'll call you Salty," Lily said.

Grandad and Lily waited for the tide to start coming in. Grandad carefully wrapped the wet towel around the baby dolphin. "Don't be scared, little Salty," said Lily. "We'll help you get back to your mummy and daddy." As the salty water crept slowly inwards, Lily and her grandad carried the dolphin out of the cave.

Salty lifted her snout and wriggled and squeaked as they waded out into the shallow sea and gently lowered her into the water. Then, with a flick of her tail, she wriggled out of the towel and swam off. "Goodbye, Salty," called Lily, feeling a little bit sad. She was happy the baby was safe, but sad to see it go.

Lily picked up her bucket. She had just started to head home when she heard
a noise. *Click-click!* Salty was back and she'd brought her family. *Splish, splash!*
The dolphins leapt in the air, twisting and turning and putting on a show.
Lily clapped and cheered. "I think they're saying thank you!" she cried.

The Treasure Hunt

"Happy birthday!" Ellie's parents called, bursting into her room and giving her a big hug. They were holding a box wrapped in shiny, pink paper. "This is for you," they said. Ellie tore off the wrapping and squealed in excitement. Inside was a beautiful, pink party dress trimmed with little hearts.

Ellie put it on and ran to look at herself in the mirror. "I love it," she said. "There's something else," said her dad. So, Ellie rummaged in the box again and found a small card. She picked it up and read it out. *Would you like present number two? Look in the place where you keep your shoes!"*

"It's a clue," said Ellie, in a puzzled voice. "I need to look in the place where I keep my shoes. I know, it must be my wardrobe!" Ellie dashed across the room. She pulled open the wardrobe doors and peered in. Sitting below her slippers, her summer sandals and her red boots, was a brand new pair of sparkly shoes!

As Ellie slipped them on, she saw another clue nestled among the shoes.
She read it aloud. *"Look downstairs for present three. It's near a picture of a tree."*
Ellie frowned as she thought for a moment. Then, she had an idea. "Come on!"
she called to her parents and raced down the stairs, two at a time.

Over the fireplace in the living room, there was a big picture of a tree.
Ellie squealed happily when she saw a glittering tiara on the mantelpiece below it,
as well as another clue. *"The final present will make your day. It's where you tidy
your toys away."* Ellie put on the tiara, closed her eyes and thought hard.
"My toy box!" she shouted. "Let's go!"

Ellie searched through her toy box, throwing teddies, dolls and picture books around as she looked. At last, at the bottom of the box, she found a tiny, sparkly package. Inside it was a silver key. "This looks like the key to the back door," she said in surprise. "I don't understand."

Ellie rushed to the back door and fitted the key into the lock. She wiggled and jiggled it until it clicked, then pushed open the door. She couldn't believe her eyes. The garden had been decorated beautifully! There were balloons and fairy lights and the table was loaded with party plates full of yummy food.

"Surprise!" shouted Ellie's friends, leaping up from behind the table.
"Happy birthday, Ellie!" they cried. Ellie couldn't stop grinning. "Thank you,"
Ellie said to her mum and dad. "It was really clever of you to think of the clues
and it's the best birthday surprise ever!"

Fairground Fun

Katy and Clare were really excited because their grandad was taking them to the fair. Although the sisters were twins, the things they liked were often very different. Katy couldn't wait to try the exciting rides, but Clare wanted to have a go on all the stalls and sideshows. "You can take it in turns to choose what we do," said Grandad.

Katy chose first. "I want to go on the giant teacup ride," she shouted, dashing towards it. Clare wasn't sure she liked the idea of twirling teacups, but she got on the ride anyway. The music jingled and the cups spun slowly round and round. Soon, both girls were squealing in delight. "That was amazing," said Katy. "It was so much fun," said Clare.

"Now it's my turn to choose," said Clare. "I'd like to go to the hall of mirrors."
Katy didn't think there was anything exciting about mirrors. Then, she saw
her reflection in one. It made her look very strange indeed and she giggled.
She was tall and stretchy and then short and squashy. The twins couldn't stop
laughing at how wiggly and wobbly they looked.

"It's my turn again," shouted Katy. "I choose the helter-skelter!" Clare was worried because the twisty slide looked very fast and slippery. Slowly, she climbed up the stairs after her sister. She sat on a mat and zoomed down, *whoosh*, landing with a bump and a giggle at the bottom. "I knew you'd like it," said Katy, happily.

"My turn now," said Clare, leading the way to the hook-a-duck stall.
"This looks boring," moaned Katy, but it wasn't! Trying to hook a shiny,
yellow duck on the end of a stick wasn't easy, but it was a lot of fun. At last, Katy
got one and Clare got one, too. "You've both won a prize." smiled the man behind
the counter, handing over two big balloons.

"Time for lunch," said Grandad. "Let's go to the hot-dog stall." The girls sat on the grass to eat. Katy chose a hot dog with extra onions and no ketchup and Clare chose one with extra ketchup and no onions. "You two always have to be different," said Grandad, laughing. "Now, we've got just enough time for one more choice each."

"I choose the ghost train!" yelled Katy, but Clare just gulped. That sounded scary. "Don't worry," said Katy. "I'll hold your hand." They climbed onto the ride and it rattled down the track. *Boo!* A ghost appeared out of the dark, making Katy jump. Clare laughed at her sister's surprised face. "You were more scared than me," she grinned.

"Can we go on it again?" asked Katy, but Clare shook her head and pointed to the coconut shy. She wanted to knock down a coconut and win a teddy, so Grandad paid for three balls. He threw the first one and Clare threw the second. The balls missed the coconut and fell on the ground with a *thunk, thunk*. "Oh, no," cried Clare.

Now it was Katy's turn. She threw her ball as hard as she could, making the coconut bounce off the stand and onto the floor. "Wow," said the stall owner in surprise. "It looks like you've won the teddy." Katy took the bear with a grin. "I'm going to give it to Clare," she said, handing it over. "She wanted it so much."

The stall holder thought Katy was very kind. "I'll tell you what," he said. "You can both have a bear." The girls were delighted. The twin bears were almost as big as they were! Cuddling them tightly, they set off for home. "Thank you for a lovely day, Grandad," said Clare and Katy. "We love the fairground."

Where's Paws?

Olivia had come to spend the day with her grandma. Usually, Grandma was happy and smiling, but today she looked sad. Olivia sat in the kitchen and drank some juice while Grandma told her what was wrong. "Paws, my cat, is missing," she sighed. Olivia gave Grandma a hug and promised to help look for Paws.

"Paws, where are you?" called Olivia, searching Grandma's house.
She looked everywhere she could think of, even in the laundry basket. There was
no sign of Paws, anywhere. "Thank you for searching," said Grandma, looking at
the open cupboards and drawers. "Why don't you go and play now?
I'm sure Paws will come back when she's ready."

93

Olivia skipped outside to play in the garden. Suddenly, she heard a rustling noise near the hedge. She peeped through the leaves and saw two bright eyes staring back at her. "Paws!" she cried, but it was just a mummy blackbird by the bush, looking for worms for her chicks.

Just then, Olivia heard another strange sound. Up above, there was a cracking, scratching noise in the tree. A fluffy tail swished this way and that.

"Is that you, Paws?" called Olivia, but it was only a mummy squirrel, feeding her babies.

I wish I could find Paws, thought Olivia. Then, she noticed something moving in the flower bed. Was it Paws? Suddenly, two sets of long ears poked up and then two little, pink noses. A mummy rabbit and her baby were busy nibbling Grandma's prized flowers! "Shoo!" said Olivia, giggling. "You mustn't eat Grandma's flowers."

Olivia was just about to give up, when she heard little mewing sounds coming from the shed. She tried the shed door, but it was locked. Olivia didn't have the key, so she ran back into the house to find her grandma. "Come quickly," she said. "I hear mewing coming from the garden shed." Olivia and her grandma hurried outside and opened the shed door.

Inside, Grandma and Olivia found Paws! She was lying in a cosy basket on an old rug and snuggled up to her tummy were five little kittens. "That old dog basket has come in very useful!" said Grandma. "I didn't know Paws was going to have babies. What a lovely surprise."

Olivia crouched down to look at Paws and her kittens. "You deserve a reward for finding Paws," said Grandma. "We'll ask your mum if you can take a kitten home when they're a bit older." Olivia was so happy she gave her grandma a hug. Wow! What an amazing day. She couldn't wait to have a kitten of her very own.

Princess World

Tilly and Helena had been looking forward to visiting Princess World for ages. They were dressed up in their princess outfits and glittery tiaras. Even Tilly's mother had put on a tiny, plastic crown. "Welcome to Princess World," beamed a lady in a sparkly dress. "Step through the gates and make your princess dreams come true!"

Princess World

Tilly and Helena stared up at her. "Are you a real princess?" Tilly whispered, pushing her glasses further up her nose, but the lady just winked and smiled. Tilly's mother paid for three tickets and the girls raced excitedly into the park. "Wow!" gasped Helena as they walked up the sweeping drive that led to the royal palace. It was beautiful, with a flag flying from every turret.

Inside the palace, everything was perfectly princessy. There were grand paintings on the walls, chandeliers hanging from the ceilings and even a pattern of crowns on the carpets. The girls explored, peeping out of windows and racing up and down the steps in the tallest tower. They both squeezed onto the throne and had their picture taken.

In the royal bedchamber, there was a huge, four-poster bed with purple bed sheets and comfy cushions. "I'd love to bounce on it," sighed Tilly. Her mother pointed to a sign that read, '*Bouncing on the bed is allowed at all times,* signed, The Princess.' "Yippee!" yelled Tilly, bouncing up and down beside Helena. "I love being a princess!"

Tilly's mother took the girls into the palace garden. They played catch around the flower beds and fed the royal swans, then took a ride in the royal carriage, drawn by four white horses. "This is fun!" said Helena. "I feel like a real princess."

"Me, too," said Tilly and she reached up to straighten her tiara, but it had gone.

"Oh, no! I've lost my tiara," gasped Tilly. The girls looked inside the coach and outside, among the flower beds, but the tiara was nowhere to be found. "Don't worry. I'll buy you another tiara," said Mum, but Tilly didn't want a new one. "My old one would have reminded me of this special day," she said, sadly.

Just then, the girls saw someone coming towards them, holding Tilly's tiara. It was the beautiful lady they had met at the entrance. "Hello," said the lady. "I am Princess Petal. I found this under my pillow. You must have lost it when you were bouncing on my bed," Helena gasped. The lady was a real princess!

"Would you like to join me for some afternoon tea?" asked Princess Petal.
"Yes, please!" replied Tilly and Helena. In the royal garden, everyone had cucumber sandwiches, royal cupcakes and a jug of fizzy lemonade.
The girls felt just like proper princesses and even Mum did, too. It had been a wonderful day in Princess World.

107

Susie's Special Cupcakes

Susie was in the kitchen with her mum and little brother, Joe. Mum was helping Susie to make cupcakes. "These are going to be perfect," said Susie, as she stirred the mixture with a wooden spoon. "Be careful," said Mum. "Don't stir too hard." Susie wasn't listening. Blobs of cake mixture flew out of the bowl and splattered onto the floor. "Yuck!" cried Joe, as he rode by on his toy tractor.

When the mixture was ready, it was time to spoon it into the cupcake cases. "Do it carefully," said Mum, but Susie picked up the spoon and started to dollop out the gloopy mixture. Some of the cases got a lot of mixture and some got hardly any. "Never mind," said Mum and she popped the cakes in the oven to bake.

While the cupcakes were cooking, Susie and her mum made a bowl of bright, pink icing. *Ping!* went the timer on the oven to say the cupcakes were baked. Mum took the hot tray out and put the cakes onto a plate. "Give them time to cool," she said, but Susie didn't want to wait. "I want to decorate them now!" she cried. Susie grabbed a spoon and dripped icing onto the hot cakes, but the icing melted and slid off the cakes onto the table.

Susie stared at the messy cupcakes. They looked nothing like the perfect ones in the cookery book. "I wanted them to be special," she said, with a small sob. Her mum gave her a hug. "You were in too much of a hurry," she said, "but things don't have to be perfect to be special. These cakes are special because you made them." Mum took a bite out of one. "Mmm! Yummy!"

Suddenly, there was a thud as Joe bumped into the table and fell off his tractor.
"Ouch," he said, starting to cry. "I hurt my knee."
"There, there," said Mum, giving him a cuddle. "Try one of Susie's extra special, yummy cupcakes. It will make you feel better." Joe took a bite of a cupcake and stopped crying. "Mmm," he said, smiling.

Just then, there was a knock at the door. It was their neighbour, Mrs Smith. "I've locked myself out of my house," she said. "Can I wait here until my son comes with a spare key? I'm feeling a bit flustered."

Susie's mum gave Miss Smith a cup of coffee and a cake. "What a delicious cake," said Mrs Smith. "I feel much better now I've eaten this. Your cupcakes are delicious, Suzie," she said.

Susie gave a little smile. She was beginning to feel better, too. "Let's all have a drink and take the cupcakes into the garden," said Mum. So, Mum made fresh lemonade and took the plate of cupcakes outside. Mrs Smith, Mum and Joe all had a second cupcake. "Mmm, delicious!" they said, laughing.

Susie picked up a cupcake and took a big bite. It was a bit lopsided and the icing wasn't neat, but it didn't matter. It really was yummy! In fact, it was the best cupcake she'd ever tasted. "The only problem with my cakes now is that they will all be eaten," she giggled. "It looks like it's time to make some more special cupcakes!"

Swimming Star

Madison was at the swimming pool, watching her big sister, Amy, take part in the swimming show. There were games and races and diving displays. Madison was so proud when her sister won a medal with a star on it. "I wish I could win a medal," she said. "You have to learn to swim first," her mum told her. "I can teach you." Madison thought that this was a very good idea indeed.

2ⁿᵈ

1ˢᵗ

3ʳᵈ

The next day, Madison's mum took her to the pool. Madison loved wearing her swimsuit and armbands, but she didn't like the cold water. It was freezing! "It's cold at first," explained her mum, "but you warm up when you get in." Suddenly, a little boy swam past, splashing water everywhere.
"Urgh!" cried Madison. "Now I'm all wet!"

Madison's mum smiled. "It's a swimming pool," she said. "You have to get wet if you want to learn how to swim." Madison let her mum help her into the water. She could just reach the bottom of the pool, but she still she held on tightly to the side. "Kick your legs and make a big splash," said her mum. "It will help you warm up."

Next, Madison's mum showed her how to move her arms. "Cup your hands and move your arms in circles, pushing the water away from you," she said. So, Madison let go of the rail and had a go. "Good job," said her mum. "I'm proud of you. Now we can have fun." She found some floats made of foam and they played a silly, splashy game together. The other children joined in too.

Every week, Madison and her mum went to the pool. Bit by bit, Madison grew more confident. Soon, she wanted to try swimming without her armbands. At first, Mum held her, but then she was kicking her feet and moving her hands like she'd been taught. Suddenly, Madison realised her mum wasn't holding her anymore. She was swimming all by herself.

"You're a real water baby," said her mum laughing. Madison loved being able to swim. After a few more lessons, she didn't even have to wear her armbands anymore. There was still one thing she wanted to do more than anything and that was to show her sister, who was away at summer camp, her new swimming skills.

On the last day of the holidays, Madison's mother planned a special secret for Madison. When they got to the pool, someone was waiting for them. It was Amy. "Surprise!" she giggled. The whole family had fun splashing and playing in the water together. Madison and Amy even had a swimming race. "I won!" yelled Madison.

After swimming, Madison's sister reached into her bag and pulled out a medal with a big star on it. "It's for being a swimming superstar," she grinned. Madison gasped. "It's just like the one you won at the show," she said. "It's even better," said her sister. "It's made out of chocolate!" Madison took a big bite. "Swimming is the best," she said, "and so is chocolate!"

The New Baby

Poppy was very excited because Mum and Dad were coming home with a new baby boy. "You're going to be a big sister," said Grandma. Just then, Mum and Dad arrived. "Hello," said Mum. "Poppy, this is your new brother, William." William was really small and cute. "I'm his big sister!" cried Poppy and everyone laughed.

Mum let Poppy hold William for just a minute. Then, everyone sat down and Grandma made a drink. "Mum is very tired," said Dad. He asked Poppy if she would like to play with William for a little bit. "Yes, please!" cried Poppy. Everyone went into the living room and William giggled and wriggled.

Poppy's dad put William down on a fluffy rug. Poppy knelt down beside him to say hello. "I'm your sister," she said. "What games do you like playing?"
William snuffled and waved his arms. "Would you like to see my toys?" she asked.
William gurgled and kicked his legs but he didn't answer.
"I'm sorry, Poppy," said her dad. "William can't talk yet."

126

Poppy's mother gave William some milk. She had just put him down in his cot to have a nap, when Poppy found her toy drum and started to play. *Rat-a-tat-tat!* "Shh, Poppy," said her mum. "Babies don't like loud noises. Especially when they're trying to go to sleep." Poppy felt a bit cross. William was spoiling all her fun.

That night, after Poppy had gone to bed, William started to cry. Poppy woke up and ran to her parents' room to see what was happening. "Don't worry, Poppy," said her mum. "Babies often wake up in the night because they are hungry." Poppy went back to bed feeling confused. She never got up in the middle of the night because she was hungry.

The next morning, Grandma helped Poppy to make cookies to welcome William. Poppy couldn't wait to give one to him, but her dad wouldn't let her feed him even the smallest bit. "Babies can't eat cookies," he said and Poppy felt upset. She had spent ages making them delicious with raisins and chocolate chips.

Poppy was very fed up. She had looked forward to having a baby brother, but now she wasn't sure. "I don't think I want a baby brother anymore," she said, sadly. "I want someone I can play with. Can you take him back and get a puppy instead?" she asked. Poppy's mother started to laugh. "William has to stay," she said, smiling, "but would you like to help me give him a bath?"

Mum put water into a baby bath and lowered William in. Poppy floated a yellow rubber duck and said, "This is for you to play with, William." Suddenly, William opened his eyes and smiled. "That's his first smile," said Mum. Poppy felt very proud, especially when her dad rushed in to see. Maybe being a big sister wasn't so bad after all.

131

The Glittery Picnic

One rainy morning, Lisa's friend, Anna, came round to play. She was dressed as a fairy princess and Anna wanted to look like one, too. Quickly, she dashed to her wardrobe and put on her own shiny wings and tiara. "Now I am Princess Flitter and you are Princess Flutter," she said happily, waving her magic wand. "We can invite all our dolls to a royal fairy picnic in the playroom!"

Dressing up

Lisa's mum helped the girls make paper fairy wings for the dolls. The friends took it in turns to add silver and pink glitter to make them sparkle.

"They look magical," said Anna. "Let's get the picnic ready."

Lisa spread out a cosy picnic blanket and cushions on the floor of the playroom. Anna added pretty cups and plates.

"Now we just need to find some fairy food," said Lisa. "I wonder what our dolls would like to eat?" The girls hunted around the playroom. Anna searched in the toy kitchen and found some strawberries, cream cakes and cheese sandwiches, all made of plastic. Lisa even spotted some erasers that looked like biscuits. "Delicious for dolls," they said, giggling.

The girls put the food on the dolls' plates and Anna waved her wand over it. "Princess Flutter welcomes you all to the fairy kingdom," she declared, grandly. "May the royal fairy feast begin!" She fetched the tubes of glitter and poured silver and pink sparkles over everything. "This is fairy dust," she whispered to Lisa, "so it looks like real fairy food."

Soon, the whole room was covered in glitter. "Now it's time for little fairies to fly home," said Lisa. She picked up her dolls and zoomed them through the air. Anna joined in and they skipped and twirled around the room until they fell into a giggling heap on the blanket. Just then, Lisa's mum opened the door. "What a glittery mess!" she gasped.

"I thought you might like some picnic food of your own," said Lisa's mum, with a smile, "but maybe without the glitter!" Both the girls giggled and sat down. There were delicious sandwiches, cookies and juice. "Yum, yum," they said. "Now we can all have a magical playtime picnic!"

The Rainy Day

Chloe looked at the rain splattering on her window and sighed. *Plip! Plop! Plip!* It was too wet to go to the park and she was feeling bored. Then, her mum popped her head around the door. "I know what you can do," she said, looking round the room with a smile. "A rainy day is the perfect time to tidy your room."

Chloe felt cross. She didn't want to tidy her room. There were piles of clothes heaped on her bed and toys dotted here and there. Some were even sticking out from under the bed. Her cushions and books were all over the floor. "It is going to take ages to tidy it all," Chloe thought with a groan.

First, Chloe collected up all her dressing-up clothes and bundled them back into the dressing-up box where they belonged. As she picked up her superhero cape and cat mask, she noticed her pink ballet tutu hiding underneath. Fantastic! She had been looking for ages. Chloe put it on and whirled and twirled around the room.

Next, Chloe began to gather up her books and put them back on the shelf.
At the bottom of the pile was a book she hadn't read for ages. It was a story about
a ballerina who turned into a superhero. Chloe sat on her beanbag to read it and it
was brilliant. As she was finishing the story, Chloe noticed something
sticking out from under her bed.

"There you are, Ragdoll!" said Chloe. She had been looking for her doll for ages. Chloe scooped her up and put her on the pillow. "I wonder what else might be under my bed," she said. Chloe got down on the floor and peered under her bed. There was her missing sock and her other bunny slipper and best of all, the missing pieces of her jigsaw puzzle. "Now I can finish the picture," said Chloe.

Next, Chloe tidied things into her toy box. She picked up her toy farm animals and her little, toy train, her soft, squeaky bunny and her box of rainbow crayons. "I think I will keep the crayons out and make a sign for my bedroom," said Chloe. So, she got a piece of pink card and decorated it, then wrote 'Chloe's Room' in big letters on it.

Mum came upstairs and smiled when she saw Chloe's bedroom. She helped her stick the card onto her door. "You've missed a word, though," she said. "It should say Chloe's *tidy* room." Chloe giggled. Tidying-up wasn't so bad because she'd found lots of things she had forgotten about. "There's something else you haven't noticed," said Mum. "It's stopped raining!"

Chloe had been having so much fun tidying up that she hadn't even noticed. "Let's go outside," said Mum and they both put on their coats and boots and went into the garden. They played all afternoon and had lots of fun. Chloe was very happy and decided that she would never mind tidying her bedroom again!

The Quiet Game

"Let's start a band!" said Rose to her sister, Alice, one day. Rose blew her whistle as hard as she could and played the keys of her toy piano. Alice giggled as she banged the drum and Ginger the cat put her paws over her ears. "Girls!" called their mum, over the loud banging, whistling and plinking. "I'm trying to do some work. Can you play something quieter, please?"

With a sigh, the girls put down their instruments and went to play outside.
At first, they were quiet, then Rose started to push Alice on the swing.
Alice shrieked excitedly as she whooshed through the air. "I'm going higher
than the trees!" she yelled. "Shush, girls!" called their mum from the house.
"That's still a bit too loud!"

Let's do some drawing," said Rose, fetching some paper. Alice drew a rocket ship blasting off into space. She picked it up and zoomed around the garden. Rose drew a dinosaur. She chased after Alice, roaring loudly. "Girls!' groaned their mother. "That's really not very quiet at all."

Rose and Alice thought for a moment. "I've got an idea," said Rose.
"Let's play a game where the quietest person wins. The first person to say or do
anything noisy is the loser." Alice nodded. So, the girls crept back into the house,
as silent as mice. They sneaked past their mother and tiptoed up the stairs
to their bedroom.

Mum worked for a while and then noticed that there wasn't a sound coming from anywhere. "It's very quiet," she said. "A bit too quiet. I wonder what Rose and Alice are up to." Mum put some snacks into a bowl and took them upstairs with some drinks. She peeked round the bedroom door and saw the girls sitting very still, looking at books. "Would you like a snack?" she asked. The girls nodded, but didn't say a word.

Alice and Rose took the snacks and drinks and sat in silence.
"Are you feeling ill?" asked Mum. The girls just shook their heads.
Suddenly, Mum guessed what was going on. "You're playing the quiet game!"
she said, laughing. The girls tried not to make a noise, but they couldn't help it.
Soon, all three were giggling helplessly.

"I'm sorry you had to be quiet," said Mum. "I missed my noisy girls
and I think I've done enough work for one day. Now it's time for some fun.
Come on, let's go downstairs."
Alice and Rose giggled and followed their mum. In the lounge,
Mum picked up one of Alice's tambourines and started to play.

Alice grabbed her big drum and Rose began tooting on her whistle and playing her toy piano. "Our band is back together," cried Alice, "and now we have an extra member!" Everyone played as loudly as they could and made lots and lots of noise. Mum didn't mind, though, because being in a girl band was the best fun ever!

Puppy Trouble

It was a bright, sunny morning. Taylor was playing outside when she heard a scrabbling noise coming from next-door's garden. She looked up and saw her friend, Annie, peeking over the fence. "Taylor!" shouted Annie, excitedly. "Come and look. Bouncer's had her puppies!" Taylor rushed to ask her mum if she could go.

In Annie's kitchen, Bouncer was lying in her basket, looking very pleased
with herself. Six cute puppies were curled up next to her. They looked so soft
and snuggly. Annie showed Taylor how to stroke them gently. "I know that your
mum said you could have one," she said, "but they have to stay with their mummy
until they are a bit older."

A few weeks later, Annie knocked on Taylor's
front door. She was holding a big cardboard box and
Taylor could hear something scratching inside it.
"It's your new puppy," grinned Annie. "Have you got
a name for him?" Taylor hadn't thought of a name yet.
She scooped up the puppy and he gave her face a
wet, sloppy lick.

Taylor giggled and the little puppy wriggled out of her arms and onto the floor.
He knocked over the laundry basket and all the washing tumbled out.
"You could call him Socks," smiled Annie, as the little puppy dashed through
the house with a yellow sock in his mouth. Taylor sprinted after him.

Taylor's cat, Lucky, was lapping water from her bowl. She gave a surprised meow when she saw the puppy hurtling towards her. She leapt up and raced out of the back door. The little puppy gave chase, knocking over the water bowl as he went. "You could call him Clumsy," said Annie, laughing.

Lucky sprang up onto the garden fence and disappeared from sight. The puppy jumped up and down, scratching at the fence and barking, excitedly. "Not the flowers," groaned Taylor, watching as he trampled over her mum's flowers. She ran over and picked him up, giving him a cuddle as she carried him back inside.

Taylor popped the puppy back into his box and Annie gave him a dog biscuit to munch. "I'm going to call you Mischief," grinned Taylor. She leaned over the side of the box and stroked the puppy's soft, little head. "It definitely suits you." Mischief looked at Taylor. He wagged his tail and woofed. "I think he likes it, too!" giggled Annie.